The Best Christmas Pageant Ever

by **BARBARA ROBINSON**

Illustrated by LAURA CORNELL

HARPER
An Imprint of HarperCollinsPublishers

This is a picture-book adaptation of the novel *The Best Christmas Pageant Ever* by Barbara Robinson.

The Best Christmas Pageant Ever

Text copyright © 2011 by Barbara Robinson

Illustrations copyright © 2011 by Laura Cornell

All rights reserved. Printed in the United States of America.

No part of this book may be used or reproduced in any manner whatsoever without written permission except in the case of brief quotations embodied in critical articles and reviews. For information address HarperCollins Children's Books, a division of HarperCollins Publishers, 10 East 53rd Street, New York, NY 10022.

www.harpercollinschildrens.com

Library of Congress Cataloging-in-Publication Data

Robinson, Barbara.

    The best Christmas pageant ever / by Barbara Robinson ; illustrated by Laura Cornell. — 1st ed.

        p.   cm.

    "A picture-book adaptation of the novel *The Best Christmas Pageant Ever*, by Barbara Robinson"—T.p. verso.

    Summary: The six horrible Herdmans, the worst children in the history of the world, take over the annual Christmas pageant.

    ISBN 978-0-06-089074-2

    [1. Christmas—Fiction. 2. Brothers and sisters—Fiction. 3. Behavior—Fiction. 4. Humorous stories.] I. Cornell, Laura, ill. II. Title.

PZ7.R5628Be3 2011   2010042666

[E]—dc22   CIP

                                                                      AC

11 12 13 14 15   LPR   10 9 8 7 6 5 4 3 2 1

❖

First Edition

For my grandsons, Tomas, Marcos, and Lucas,
who are readers and writers and actors and artists—beloved boys
—B.R.

To the spirit of my family, the Cornells and the Pells,
and to the spirit of the Herdmans
—L.C.

RALPH
10

IMOGENE
9

LEROY
8

CLAUDE
7

OLLIE
6

GLADYS
5

The Herdmans were the worst kids in the history of the world.
They lied and stole and played with matches.
They were so awful, you could hardly believe they were real.

There were six of them—Ralph, Imogene, Leroy, Claude, Ollie, and Gladys.
They were skinny and stringy haired and dirty and all different sizes, with all
different black-and-blue places where they had clonked each other.

They lived over a garage, and when they didn't have anything else to do, they would bang the garage door up and down and try to squash each other . . . or the mailman . . . or their crazy one-eyed cat. Everybody stayed away from them.

Then one day they showed up in Sunday school. They stole all the money out of the collection plate and drew mustaches on everybody in the Bible.
And, though nobody knows how, they took over our annual Christmas pageant.

ANGEL WINGS

SHEPHE TOWELS and SHOWER CAPS

Our Christmas pageant is always the same—kids in bathrobes and bed sheets,
acting out the story of Mary, Joseph, and the Baby Jesus being born.
Everybody knows the story . . . everybody but the Herdmans.

That didn't stop them from picking out the best parts for themselves.

"I'll be the Mary," Imogene yelled, "and Ralph, he'll be the Joseph."

Everyone else was afraid to volunteer.

That left three Herdmans—Leroy, Claude, and Ollie—to be Wise Men, and the worst Herdman of them all to be the Angel of the Lord. "Me!" Gladys hollered. "I'll be that. . . . What is it?"

So then somebody had to read the whole story to them—about the star and the shepherds, and how "there was no room at the inn . . ." and how "the Baby Jesus slept in a manger."

The Herdmans were shocked.

"They stuck them out in the barn?" Imogene yelped. "And they tied Jesus up in rags and put him in a feed box! At least we put Gladys in a bureau drawer!"

Then they heard about the Wise Men bringing gifts of oil and frankincense.
Claude said, "What good is smelly oil? If we're the Wise Men, let's bring pizza."

Every year someone lent us their baby to be Jesus. Not this year. Nobody would trust a Herdman with their baby, so Imogene offered to steal one from the supermarket. "There's always babies in carts there," she said.

"Umm, let's forget about a baby," someone said.

We used a doll instead.

Every rehearsal was an adventure. Leroy wanted to chase the mean innkeeper out of town, and Claude and Ollie wanted to run off with the baby to keep him safe.

Imogene said she wouldn't name him Jesus. She would name him Bill, and she wouldn't let the Wise Men worship him.

"Get away from that baby!" she barked at them. "You might have germs."

When Gladys found out the Angel of the Lord appeared out of nowhere in the black of night, she was sure it was out of Amazing Comics.

"Shazam!" she yelled, smacking the kid next to her. Gladys liked to smack things.

Our Mary was loud and bossy, the Wise Men were sneaky, and the Angel of the Lord came from outer space. This was going to be the worst Christmas pageant ever.

Some people wanted to cancel the whole thing.

The minister said, "I don't think *anyone* will come to see it."

But they were all wrong. Everybody came . . . just to see what the Herdmans would do.

When the curtain opened, Ralph and Imogene stood in the wings, frozen, as if they weren't sure what to do. They weren't pushing or hitting or being Herdmans. The chorus waited and hummed, hummed and waited, like an old refrigerator.

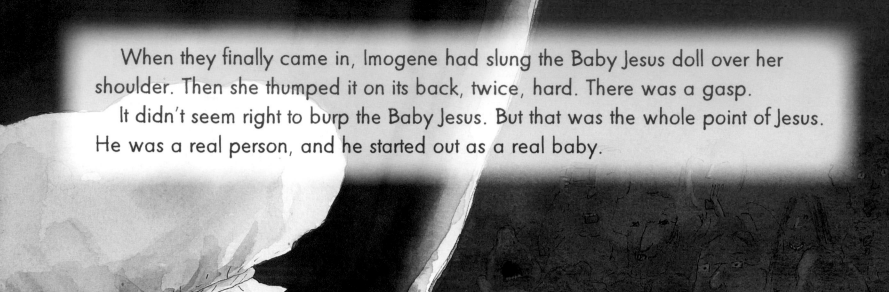

When they finally came in, Imogene had slung the Baby Jesus doll over her shoulder. Then she thumped it on its back, twice, hard. There was a gasp.

It didn't seem right to burp the Baby Jesus. But that was the whole point of Jesus. He was a real person, and he started out as a real baby.

His parents were real, too . . . as real as Imogene, with her veil all crooked, and Ralph, with his hair sticking out, as if they had slept in their clothes, out in the barn. Just like in the real story.

Then came Gladys from behind the shepherds, shoving them out of the way and stepping on everyone's feet.

"Hey!" she yelled. "Unto you a child is born! He's in the barn!"

She made it sound like it was the best news in the world.

Right behind Gladys came the Wise Men, but they didn't have the usual frankincense and gold and oil . . . and they didn't have a pizza.

Instead, Leroy was carrying something big and heavy.

It was a ham from the Herdmans' food basket. The church gave them one every year. The Herdmans had never before given anything away except clonks on the head, so you had to be impressed. The Herdmans were giving the Baby Jesus their Christmas ham!

Then the Wise Men were supposed to leave and go home, but instead they just sat down. Actually, it seemed like the right thing to do. After all, they had come a long way, and you wouldn't expect them just to hand over the ham and leave.

It seemed natural, too, to burp a baby who might be fussy or tired, and for someone to tell people where the baby was so they wouldn't have to wander all over the place. Somehow every wrong thing the Herdmans did seemed right and natural.

And then, as everyone sang "Silent Night," Imogene started to cry.
In the candlelight her face was all shiny with tears—awful old Imogene, in her crookedy veil, crying as if Christmas had just come over her all at once.

When everyone left the church that night, it was cold and clear, with crunchy snow underfoot and bright, bright stars in the sky.

Everyone said there was something different this time, something special. And though nobody could say exactly what that something was, everyone agreed. . . .

It was the best Christmas pageant ever!